MADELINE
ACTIVITY BOOK WITH STICKERS

based on the characters created by Ludwig Bemelmans

Grosset & Dunlap
An Imprint of Penguin Group (USA) Inc.

GROSSET & DUNLAP
Published by the Penguin Group
Penguin Group (USA) Inc., 375 Hudson Street, New York, New York 10014, USA
Penguin Group (Canada), 90 Eglinton Avenue East, Suite 700, Toronto, Ontario M4P 2Y3, Canada
(a division of Pearson Penguin Canada Inc.)
Penguin Books Ltd., 80 Strand, London WC2R 0RL, England
Penguin Group Ireland, 25 St. Stephen's Green, Dublin 2, Ireland
(a division of Penguin Books Ltd.)
Penguin Group (Australia), 250 Camberwell Road, Camberwell, Victoria 3124, Australia
(a division of Pearson Australia Group Pty. Ltd.)
Penguin Books India Pvt. Ltd., 11 Community Centre, Panchsheel Park, New Delhi—110 017, India
Penguin Group (NZ), 67 Apollo Drive, Rosedale, Auckland 0632, New Zealand
(a division of Pearson New Zealand Ltd.)
Penguin Books (South Africa) (Pty.) Ltd., 24 Sturdee Avenue,
Rosebank, Johannesburg 2196, South Africa

Penguin Books Ltd., Registered Offices: 80 Strand, London WC2R 0RL, England

The publisher does not have any control over and does not assume any
responsibility for author or third-party websites or their content.

The contents of this book first appeared in *Madeline Playtime Activity Book*, *Madeline Christmas Activity Book*, and
Madeline Birthday Activity Book, with art by Jody Wheeler, published by Viking Books, copyright © 1997, 1998,
1999 by Penguin Group (USA) Inc. All rights reserved. *Madeline*, *Madeline's Rescue*, *Madeline and the Bad Hat*, and
Madeline's Christmas copyright © 1939, 1951, 1956, 1956 by Ludwig Bemelmans. Copyright renewed.

Published in 2012 by Grosset & Dunlap, a division of Penguin Young Readers Group, 345 Hudson Street, New York,
New York 10014. GROSSET & DUNLAP is a trademark of Penguin Group (USA) Inc. Manufactured in China.

ISBN 978-0-448-45903-5   10 9 8 7 6 5 4 3

MADELINE

Stories and pictures by
Ludwig Bemelmans

In an old house in Paris that was covered with vines

lived twelve little girls in two straight lines.

In two straight lines they broke their bread

and brushed their teeth and went to bed.

They smiled at the good and frowned at the bad

and sometimes they were very sad.

They left the house at half past nine

in two straight lines in rain or shine—

the smallest one was Madeline.

She was not afraid of mice—she loved winter, snow, and ice.

To the tiger in the zoo

Madeline just said, "Pooh-pooh,"

and nobody knew so well how to frighten Miss Clavel.

In the middle of one night

Miss Clavel turned on her light

and said, "Something is not right!"

Little Madeline sat in bed, cried and cried; her eyes were red.

And soon after Dr. Cohn

came, he rushed out to the phone

and he dialed: DANton-ten-six—

"Nurse," he said, "it's an appendix!"

Everybody had to cry—not a single eye was dry.

Madeline was in his arm in a blanket safe and warm.

In a car with a red light they drove out into the night.

Madeline woke up two hours

later, in a room with flowers.

Madeline soon ate and drank.

On her bed there was a crank,

and a crack on the ceiling had the habit

of sometimes looking like a rabbit.

Outside were birds, trees, and sky—

and so ten days passed quickly by.

One nice morning Miss Clavel said—

"Isn't this a fine—

day to visit Madeline."

VISITORS FROM TWO TO FOUR

read a sign outside her door.

Tiptoeing with solemn face,

with some flowers and a vase,

in they walked and then said, "Ahhh,"

when they saw the toys and candy and the dollhouse from Papa.

But the biggest surprise by far—*on her stomach was a scar!*

"Good-by," they said, "we'll come again,"

and the little girls left in the rain.

They went home and broke their bread
brushed their teeth and went to bed.
In the middle of the night
Miss Clavel turned on the light
and said, "Something is not right!"
And afraid of a disaster
Miss Clavel ran fast and faster,
and she said, "Please children do—
tell me what is troubling you?"
And all the little girls cried, "Boohoo,
we want to have our appendix out, too!"
"Good night, little girls!
Thank the lord you are well!
And now go to sleep!"
said Miss Clavel.
And she turned out the light—
and closed the door—
and that's all there is—
there isn't any more.

Color in the picture.

Learn how to draw Madeline!

STEP 1:
Draw her head.

STEP 2:
Add her face.

STEP 3:
Add her hat.

STEP 4:
Add the top of her hat.

STEP 5:
Add her hair.

STEP 6:
Add her dress.

STEP 7:
Add her collar and buttons.

STEP 8:
Add her arms and hands.

STEP 9:
Add her legs, shoes, and socks.

Draw Madeline here.

Fill in the blanks.

M _ _ _ _ _ _ _ _ _

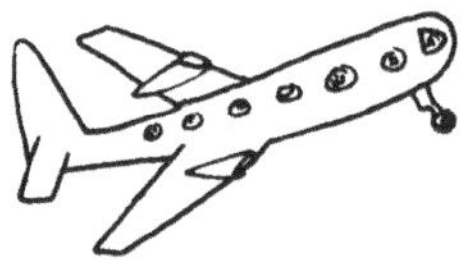

A _ _ _ _ _ _ _

D _ _

E _ _

L _ _ _

I _ _ _ _ _ _ _

N _ _ _ _

E _ _ _ _ _ _ _ _ _

10

Madeline's dog, Genevieve, is lost!
Help Madeline find her.

Can you find the objects below
hidden on the next page?

Circle the words hidden in the puzzle below.

tent

gypsy

horse

popcorn

```
G I R L S A T S
Y C L H D O E H
P O P C O R N H
S W O L G R T R
Y N P O C Y S S
C L O W M S N E
Z U R N D G O G
A G C M A P S Y
```

clown

girls

dog

Can you decode the picture reader below?

Solve the crossword puzzle.

Across:

3.

5.

6.

7.

Down:

1.

2.

4.

Learn how to draw the clown from Madeline and Pepito's circus!

STEP 1:
Draw his hat.

STEP 2:
Add his head and face.

STEP 3:
Add his collar.

STEP 4:
Add his shirt.

STEP 5:
Add his arms and hands.

STEP 6:
Add his legs and shoes.

STEP 7:
Decorate his costume.

STEP 8:
Color in sections of his costume.

STEP 9:
Add his juggling balls.

Draw the clown here.

Help Miss Clavel find Madeline and Pepito at the circus.

Start here

Can you tell which two Pepitos are not like the others?
Circle them.

Color by number.

1. Gray   2. Yellow   3. Purple   4. Light Blue   5. Orange

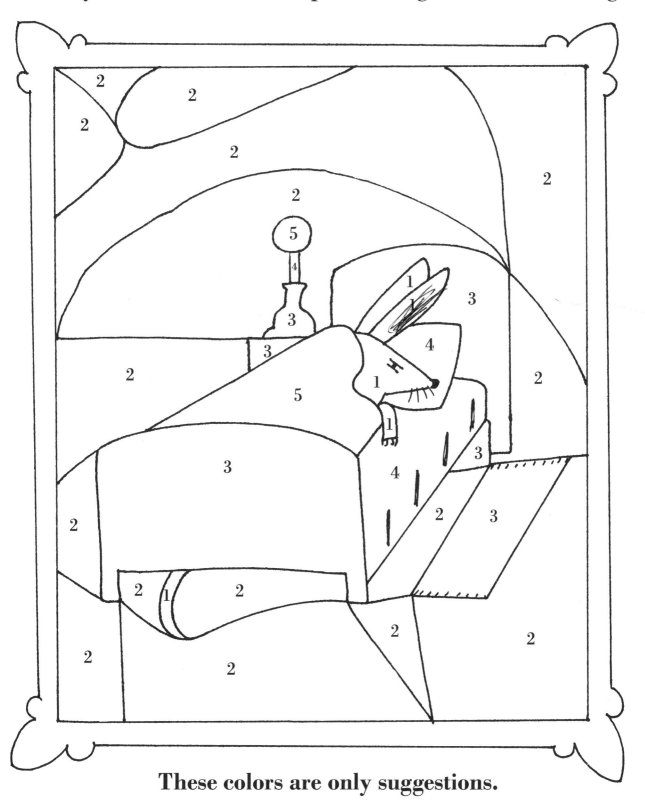

These colors are only suggestions.

And it's okay to color outside the lines, too.

Can you find the objects below hidden on the next page?

Find the picture in each row that is different from the others.

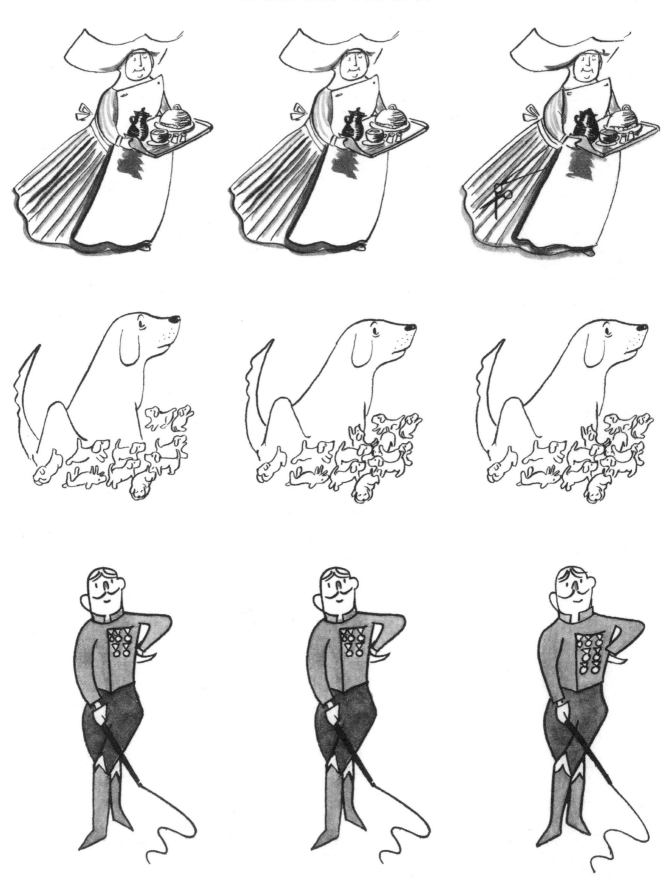

Match the item in the left column with the place where it belongs in the right column.

Can you find five mice hidden in the picture below?

Connect the dots.

Circle the words hidden in the puzzle below.

moon

flowers

tent

farmer

```
Z D N U S F L P
E L E P H A N T
W R I G T R R E
D C Y O Q M A N
K M O O N E B T
F L O W E R S A
```

elephant

lion

barn

cow

Answers

Page 10

M iss Clavel

A irplane

D og

E ye

L ion

I ce skate

N urse

E iffel Tower

Page 14

```
G I R L S A T S Y
Y C L H D O E H
P O P C O R N H
S W O L G R T R
Y N P O C Y S S
C L O W M S N E
Z U R N D G O G
A G C M A P S Y
```

Pages 16–17

```
        2
        M
  1     A
  T   3 D
  I G E N E V I E V E      4
3 G     L           5      P
  E   5 M I S S C L A V E L
  R     I                  P
6 T R E E                  I
                           T
                7 D O C T O R
```

Page 22

Answers

Page 26

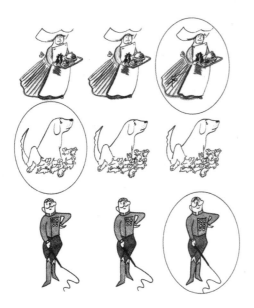

Page 27

Page 30

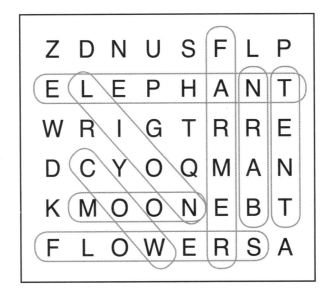